DINOSAUR PIE

Jen Wallace

Little
Island

DINOSAUR PIE

First published in 2024 by
Little Island Books
7 Kenilworth Park
Dublin 6w
Ireland

First published in the USA by Little Island in 2025

A British Library Cataloguing in Publication record for this
book is available from the British Library.

Cover design and typesetting by Niall McCormack
Proofread by Emma Dunne
Printed in Poland by L&C

Print ISBN: 9781915071491

Little Island has received funding to support this book from
the Arts Council of Ireland / An Chomhairle Ealaíon

10 9 8 7 6 5 4 3 2 1

For Róisín, Kirin and Tigey Cat,
with love, always

MORNING CHAOS

I'm Rory, sometimes Roary Rory, and this is the story of the weirdest week of my life. Well, the weirdest week so far. Probably. I mean the week I was born was probably quite weird for me. But, I don't remember that. Thankfully.

Anyway, **SPOILER ALERT**, this week's weirdness starts on Monday, when I am accidentally turned into a dinosaur. Mum blames herself, but it isn't really her fault. It all happens later in the day so we'll come back to it.

Right now, it's 6:30AM, two hours before school, and Mum is trying to wake me. She used to wake me one and a half hours before school, but we are trying two hours now, to see if it is Less Stressful. It seems to mean that I get half an hour less sleep and everything is still its usual disaster, but for slightly longer.

At this stage I totally don't appreciate the fact that I am still a human.

Anyway, I can't wake properly. I am deep in happy sleepy land. It took me ages to go asleep last night because all I could think about was the *Big Battle World* update.

Now, I'm tired and my bed is lovely and warm. It's totally not fair that I have to leave it.

When I do eventually get up, I'm apparently 'already late for school'. How can I be already late when school hasn't even started yet? I'm running to catch up again – welcome to my life.

Getting dressed is delayed just a teensy bit as I take a sneak peek at *Big Battle World*. Today is update day, the Doom Dimension update. Today the Doom Boss and the Blethers arrive and loads of other cool stuff. If you don't know what I'm talking about, *Big Battle World*, *BigB* for short, is an awesome computer game. I have been waiting for this update since they announced it three months ago and it was due to happen about midnight our time. While Mum is in the shower, I turn on the computer and have a peek. I've got to check it out so that I can tell Daria and Oleg about it later at school. Knowledge is power, people!

Mum comes out of the shower. She says, 'Rory, sweetie, hurry up. We need to be gone in forty minutes.'

Oops.

I spend ten minutes searching our flat for shoes that I had chucked somewhere yesterday. They have amazingly made their own way to the shoe rack. But I can't find socks. Bad socks! I eventually locate two similar enough to pass as a pair. They are part of the pile of clean clothes that I meant to put away, but that only got as far as the end of my bed, fell off and now lives on the floor.

Then I find my lunchbox is still in my schoolbag from Friday. Double oops. Mum says it's a biohazard. It is not as bad as the dried-out, shrivelled black banana I found when I took my schoolbag out at the end of the summer break. Mum is losing all sense of perspective.

She is now totally stressed off her head that she will be late for work. She cannot be late for work. There will be dire consequences. She is talking loud and fast, and I only have time to eat a few spoonfuls of my Oaty Krunch. I brush my teeth super fast, twice because I forgot to last night. Then it's off out the door to my favourite place in the whole world.

Only joking. It's not really my favourite place. I'm trying out sarcasm here. What do you think? I probably spoiled it by explaining it.

JUST ANOTHER NORMAL DAY, SO FAR ...

At school I can't wait to talk to my friends about the update, but I don't get a chance before class, as I am slightly late. I make our 'talk later' sign to Daria on the opposite side of the room as I take my seat next to Oleg. We can't help it – at every opportunity we are whispering. We are both terrible at whispering, like we get really loud when we are excited, and we keep nearly getting caught.

'The Blethers seems tricky,' I say quietly behind my hand. 'They look like spiders, but they can squirt lava.'

'One star for name choice, but four stars for lava-squirting ability,' says Oleg. 'I wonder what weapons we'll need to defeat them.'

'I'm not sure,' I whisper. 'I didn't get a chance to check out their weaknesses. I only had a few minutes and I didn't even get to see the Doom Boss.'

Meanwhile at school we are supposed to be listening to something about some Industrial Revolution that happened about a million years ago. Who cares?

Well, One-Two cares and he is going very red in the face and keeps glaring at Oleg and me. Who is One-Two? One-Two is our nickname for our super teacher (see that sarcasm again), Mr Jim Buckley.

One-Two, get it? No? It's an Oleg joke. I'll tell it like Oleg does.

'Mr Buckley = One Two buckle my shoe …. Boom, boom! Like and Subscribe.'

Then Oleg gives the thumbs-up sign.

Then Daria and I usually give the thumbs-down sign and sometimes pretend to vomit. I know, it's terrible. Don't blame me – I am only quoting Oleg. Oleg treats life like he's livestreaming, hence the continuous Like and Subscribe suggestions. I'm waiting for him to start advertising Oleg-themed merch soon. So, where are we?

Oh, yes. First One-Two splits us up and puts us into different project groups. This is his divide-and-conquer strategy. I am so not into the project discussion today. I have no idea what a Spinning Jenny is and I have no interest in recreating weaving techniques with strips of coloured paper. Worst of all, nobody in my group is interested in talking about *Big Battle World*.

I start feeling sleepy and rest my head on my crossed arms on the desk in front of me.

'Rory! Are you having a NAP? In my class?' One-Two bellows.

And then it happens. My chest suddenly tightens and I feel trapped. Words start to spin around in my head and everything is too bright and too loud. Here we go again.

GLITCH

Words are bashing and bumping around my brain. They have sharp edges. I wish everyone would just shut up and leave me alone. I clutch my head and stomp my feet hard on the floor. I need to run away. I need to scream. I can't do either here, so I rock and stamp. When One-Two points to the door I run out. I just pace up and down the corridor, trying to walk myself out of my head. I hate when this happens. I bang the wall and hurt my hand. My chest is tight, my jaw is clenched, and all around me are classrooms full of people, walls, closed doors. **WALLS**.

I shake it out then, walk and shake it out. I slide to the floor and hug my knees.

All kids get overwhelmed. I get overwhelmed a lot. Mum says ADHD stands for my Amazing Dynamic Hyper Disposition. Now, when I'm stressed, I think it stands for Annoying Dopey Huge Difference. Don't tell anyone, but when I was younger and first found out about my ADHD I called myself **ALEX DANGER, HUMAN DYNAMO**.

By break time I am tired but calmer and able to hang out with Daria and Oleg. Since the new principal started they don't make me stay in on break times after a meltdown or an 'episode'. Which is much better, 'cause I need to get outside and just not be in a chair for a bit.

'You OK, Rory?' asks Daria.

'Yup, just a glitch,' I reply.

ALEX DANGER, HUMAN DYNAMO

He's Super Fast.

He defies bedtimes.

He loves to spin.

He can run all day.

He's Super Awesome.

He just keeps going.

Drawing by Rory, age 4

Words by Mum

OK, this is totally embarrassing. I don't know why it's in this book. I can't believe Mum kept this.

THE ULTIMATE PLAN

'Daria, I saw the Blethers,' I say. We are in the yard at break.

'Me too,' she says, flicking back her hair annoyingly. 'And I saw the Doom Boss. He's going to be tough to defeat, but I have some ideas.'

'Woah, you've seen the Doom Boss?' says Oleg. 'For real?'

'Yup, I was online from five,' says Daria, as she stifles a yawn.

We stare at her in awe. The black shadows under her eyes indicate she is telling the truth. Daria has lots of teenage brothers, like about three or something, and the rules of her house are very different to the rest of ours, especially Oleg's.

'Online from five,' says Oleg in wonder. 'Do you think we could swap parents? I am cruelly cursed with parents who don't understand how technology will make Oleg rich and famous. YouTube is crying out for Oleg. The internet is one Oleg short of being totally awesome. Like and Subsc–'

'Oleg! *Big Battle World*. Plans. Focus. Lunch break is almost over,' Daria says. 'You only get an hour to play later, so we need a good plan. A plan that will take down that boss for ever.'

'A plan that is the Ultimate Plan!' I add in my narrator voice.

So, we come up with a plan quickly. And with barely any arguments. Well, maybe a few.

For context, the Doom Boss is this huge squid-like being, black and red, and he has a weapon in each tentacle and he is supposed to be totally fierce. Daria and I will target three tentacles each and Oleg will take the other two. We'll have to overcome the Blethers first too so we are just going to charge them as that is all we can think of. It might sound a bit basic, but it is as ultimate as we can get during lunch.

The bell goes. Break is over way too quickly, and I only ate half a sandwich.

The afternoon is totally annoying, as expected.

So here I am getting through the school day, thinking everything is going to be exactly the same tomorrow. Just blah blah, until I can get home. Then, repeat.

I am so wrong.

DINOSAUR PIE

When I get home, Mum's having a nap. She doesn't sleep so well at night so she often has a nap after work. I throw off my shoes and coat and leave my bag in my room. I grab a juice from the fridge. Then I power up the PC and pop on my headphones.

We don't have a gaming console. Gran bought us this PC as she thought it would be educational. It's OK – *BigB* is compatible with PCs. Mum is pretty chilled about gaming. I can game when I come home, so long as I get my homework done at some stage. Which I mostly do.

Daria is online so we check out the new features in the update until Oleg can join us. He does his homework first and comes online at five.

Now it's time to implement the Ultimate Plan.

Our Blethers strategy actually works. We gear ourselves up with as many weapons as we can carry and just run at them full tilt, blasting away, all of us on the voice call shouting together, 'Get the Blethers!' It's totally hilarious, and I can hear Oleg's mum in the background come running in to check if he is OK. He mutes for a bit, then he comes back and joins us.

I am so totally in it that I barely hear Mum come over. She kisses me on the hair. I give her a thumbs-up and she heads off to do her stuff.

At 6PM Oleg's tech time is up and we have not defeated the Doom Boss. We totally underestimated his strength and only got his Boss Bar down about 10 per cent. (For you noobs – the Boss Bar shows how much life-force the boss has left.) He totally murdered us. At least we got past the Blethers, though. We need to come up with a new boss plan tomorrow. The Ultimate Plan has failed. Bad, bad plan.

Mum hasn't told me it's time to come off the PC, so I concentrate on doing a few tasks in *BigB* that will help me level up. I'm at Level 36, Daria is at 39, and Oleg is at Level 27.

A while later Mum taps me on the shoulder. I lift my headset off one ear.

'Ten minutes to dinner, sweetie,' she says. 'Finish up and wash your hands.'

Then, as I'm putting my headset back, she adds, 'It's dinosaur pie.'

As I do a quick check on my inventory it registers what Mum has just said. Maybe I heard it wrong.

'What did you say, Mum?'

'I said there's dinosaur pie for dinner.'

I Save and Exit the game.

'Wait ... what?' I ask. 'Like, made from dinosaurs?'

She is pottering around singing to herself. I know she's not really ignoring me. She just gets distracted.

'Is it real dinosaur meat?' I ask. 'Where did you even get dinosaur? Aren't they extinct? Do you mean chicken pie? They evolved from dinosaurs. Didn't they? Is it chicken pie?'

'Nope. Definitely dinosaur pie,' she says. 'Too busy to talk now. Wash those hands and we eat in five minutes.'

WHAT THE HECK?

I get up to wash my hands. Can it be true? Dinosaur pie? Usually Monday dinner is sausages or chicken nuggets. What if Mum only *thinks* it's dinosaur? Maybe it's like those burgers that got recalled. Maybe BuyMart have listed the ingredients wrong again. Or maybe dinosaurs never went extinct. Maybe all the media reporting is false **AND IT'S A CONSPIRACY!** Jebey, our neighbour, is always talking about conspiracies. He says that aliens keep landing on Earth, but the government covers it up. He says he has seen real aliens. He claims he sat beside one on the bus to Dublin.

'Dinner, Rory,' Mum calls.

Oops, forgot to wash my hands.

'Be there in a minute!'

I sit down at the table. The pie in front of me looks very ordinary, like any pie from BuyMart. Mum has put peas on the side. I like peas, but they are best eaten frozen straight from the bag.

'Smells good,' I say, poking at it a bit. 'What type of dinosaur is it, Mum?'

'I'm not sure, sweetie. I threw out the label. It looks nice, though.'

'Diplodocus maybe?' It's the only herbivore I can think of.

'Mmm, hmm.' Which is Mum's way of saying that she's not really listening.

'Can't be pterosaur anyway, Mum.'

'No?'

'Nope, they're not dinosaurs!'

'Really? Hmm.'

That's most of my dinosaur knowledge used up. I used to like dinosaurs and all that, but I was never totally **INTO** dinosaurs. Not like Daria. She was obsessed with that show *Dinosaur Moon* when we were, like, six, and she knows seriously weird facts about them. I'll ask her later.

Mum is having a salad. It's just me having pie, so I muster up some courage and take my first bite. Mmm. Tastes OK. Not too stringy or gross. Actually, I quite like it. It's totally delicious. I devour the whole lot. I hadn't realised how starving I am.

Wait a minute. I feel weird. And tired, so tired.

'Are you OK, Rory?' Mum glances over. 'You are looking a bit green.'

'Don't feel so good,' I mumble. 'Need to go lie down.'

I make it to my bed. I am wiped. I need to sleep. My eyes won't stay open. I feel Mum pull my duvet over me and then I'm asleep.

It must be days before I wake, but it's still bright outside and I can hear kids playing on the green. I go to roll over but something is terribly wrong. I try to grab the duvet, but these aren't my hands. I scream, but it doesn't come out. Just a 'graagh' sound. Maybe I'm still in a horrible dream. How do I wake myself up?

I try to get out of bed, but my arms are more like wings and I am covered in feathers in what appear to be brown and grey stripes. I have scaly legs and one huge claw and three smaller ones where my feet should be. I think I may have turned into an ostrich or a giant chicken, until I become aware of the huge tail, almost the length of

the bed, behind me. My breath is fast and I can feel my heart thump-thumping away.

I make my way to the mirror on the back of my door. I am slightly shorter than usual and the face looking back at me has huge long square jaws with serious teeth. The face looks like some kind of weird feathered snake-alligator. *My* face, I realise.

DO NOT SEEK
MEDICAL ADVICE

Mum comes in. She doesn't scream – she just stands at the door and goes white.

'Rory?' she says very quietly,

I nod my big head. I feel like crying but no tears come. Maybe these eyes don't do that.

Then she says, 'Dinosaur pie.'

She tucks her hair behind her ear and goes into crisis mode. 'Come on, I need to get you to the doctor. No, sit there a minute, don't move.'

She walks quickly towards the kitchen. 'Where is that label?'

I follow her, banging into walls and doors as I go. I walk differently and I seem to need to move my huge tail to keep my balance.

Mum is frantically going through the rubbish as I try out my new jaws.

GNASH GNASH

'Here it is,' she says and reads the label:

Dinosaur Pie

Ingredients: Classified.

CAUTION: MAY CAUSE DINOSAUR TRANSFORMATION. EFFECTS SHOULD WEAR OFF IN 12 HOURS. DO NOT SEEK MEDICAL ADVICE.

We both stand there in a kind of stunned silence.

Then she puts an arm around me. 'Oh sweetie, I'm so sorry. It was on special offer in BuyMart. I thought it would be a nice change, and I didn't check the small print on the label.'

Putting on her fake-cheerful smile she adds, 'It says it will wear off in twelve hours, so you'll be a kid again by morning.'

I can't answer. Of course I can't – I can't even talk. I try to roar, but it comes out as more of a 'graagh'.

Just then there's a knock on the door and Mum waves for me to get out of sight. I scamper down to my room.

I hear, 'Hello, Rebecca. Is Rory coming out? He said he was, like, and we've been waiting for ages.'

'Oh, Daria, ehm, something has happened. He's not well.'

Daria! She's exactly who I need. Before Mum can get rid of her, I come careening around the corner, trying to stabilise myself with tail swishes and arm-wing flaps.

Daria just stands there, staring. Her mouth really does drop open, which is quite cool as I've never seen it happen in real life.

'Rebecca,' she says. 'Why is there a Deinonychus in your kitchen?'

FRIENDS ARE
NOT FOR EATING

So, Mum explains to Daria about the pie and shows her the label. I'm expecting sympathy and support.

'This is so cool!' says Daria. 'Do you have any more pie, Rebecca?'

'No, Daria, and I'm not sure it would be a good idea,' says Mum.

'Where did you even get the pie?' asks Daria.

'BuyMart,' says Mum.

'I'll text Andy,' says Daria. 'He works at BuyMart. He might be able to get us some more.'

She taps away on her phone, messaging

her older brother. I don't have a phone. Daria has had one since she was eight! I will be getting one when I turn thirteen, Mum says. That feels so far away. But for now, I don't have fingers anyway.

Eventually Daria turns to me, presumably worried about her friend's well-being.

'Can you talk?'

I squawk a bit in reply.

'No,' she says. 'Then your voice box and all must be changed.'

She plucks a feather from my wing-arm.

Ow, I snap in her direction. She doesn't seem too bothered.

'Symmetrical feather,' she says, nodding. 'Figures.'

'Give me a look at the claw,' she says, and bends down to examine my feet.

'Oh, fierce,' she says admiringly.

She looks at Mum. 'Are you sure there's no more pie?'

Mum rolls her eyes and then goes searching for something on her phone.

'Do you think you can climb with that claw or is it more for gripping and tearing?' asks Daria. 'How much dexterity do you have in your manual claws? Your hands?'

Daria is going to be running experiments on me if I don't put a stop to this. I stomp my feet, which causes some unexpected tail-swishing and some accidental crashing and smashing of bowls and plates.

At least it stops Daria for a bit.

Mum pushes her hair behind her ear, which is usually a sign that she has had enough and is ready for some decisive action. I prepare to receive orders.

'Well, you can't stomp around here

for the evening. The neighbours will all complain about the noise. Off out you go now for a play.'

But, Mum, I'm a dinosaur, I want to say.

Maybe she picks it up by telepathy, because she says, 'It'll be fine, love.'

On the way out the door of my flat, Daria gives me what she considers useful tips. 'So, Rory,' she says, 'you know you are a carnivore, right?'

I have a little think.

Could I eat a salad? Nope. An apple? Nope. Sausages? Oh yeah.

I nod enthusiastically.

She stops and gives me her serious face. 'Friends are not for eating.'

I nod my agreement.

'In fact,' she says, 'all humans are off the menu!'

Again, I nod my agreement. Does she think I am totally irresponsible?

'And those are not wings.' She prods my wing-arms. 'You do not have flight feathers.'

I give an experimental flap.

'Do **NOT** try to fly!' she says.

The thought had only briefly crossed my mind.

DOES ANYONE ELSE THINK THIS IS WEIRD?

Daria seems to be really enjoying talking without me interrupting her, punching her in the arm or just tuning her out. Yes, we are good friends, but we don't have to listen to everything each other says!

'You are not that much smaller than normal, Rory. You could be dressed up. Like in a really fancy costume. Like cosplay. Like you could totally pretend to be cosplaying a dinosaur. Like that's funny, a dinosaur playing a human cosplaying a dinosaur.'

If I have to be a dinosaur for a bit, why can't I be huge and awesome like a

Triceratops or a T Rex or some other fierce-looking one? What good is it being a small, feathered dinosaur?

Daria is still talking. I hear other voices; my hearing is super sharp now. Ah, it's just Bex, Hex and Lex, our local teenage goths, hanging out in the stairwell. They lurk in shadow and shade and are mostly harmless. I'm not totally sure what the whole goth thing is about, but they wear lots of black, have big black hair and black-and-white make-up. I would not describe them as enthusiastic, chatty, chirpy or cheerful. But neither are they mean or rude. As I said, mostly harmless.

I try to roar as we go past, but a strangled 'graagh' is all I can manage.

They don't even look our way. Giant mushrooms could sprout up and flocks of unicorns could cover the whole world in glitter and they would probably just be bored by it.

'Graagh,' I shout at Jebey, our downstairs neighbour, who is standing on a chair cleaning his windows as I stomp past. He has his hair tied up in a huge bun, his sleeves rolled up, and suds are pouring everywhere as he works the squeegee around the window. He waves with his other hand.

He doesn't seem the slightest bit surprised or concerned by my appearance. I suppose when you live here long enough you get to see a lot of weird stuff.

The sound of his window squeegee is ridiculously loud, though. What the heck? How can Jebey bear that? I run to the green to get away from it. But it's noisy there too. It sounds like we are next to a runway, but it's just Church Road with the normal traffic. These dino ears are too good. And my eyesight is weird too. I have to turn my head when I want to see things properly. It's like my eyes are stuck somehow: either they don't move by themselves or I need to figure out how to make them do it. And everything is sharper. It's hard to explain, but it's kind of like I was looking from behind foggy glass before and now the glass is gone and everything is so sharp and interesting. My head is darting about trying to see everything.

'You OK?' asks Daria.

I want to say that this is amazing, that everything is so clear and bright, but also really loud and intense. Every time a noise startles me, my head jerks in that direction and my feathers rise. It is really weird to feel your own feathers move. I suppose it must be like when cats fluff up to look big. I have a giggle to myself imagining if human hair could do that. Like they draw it in animation sometimes. I just nod that I'm OK and give what I hope is a friendly 'graagh'.

'Okaaay,' says Daria. 'Let's go find Oleg. I left him at the half wall, with my phone to keep him busy.'

The half wall is where we like to hang out. It is on the other side of the green. You can't see it from my end because of the trees in the middle. We don't hang out by the trees. Weird and icky stuff happens there sometimes, so we have our fallen-down bit of wall that we call the half wall.

I spot Oleg at our place. Any other day, he is my friend. But today, he is ...

PREY!

PREY

I gnash and flap and run at Oleg. I'm not actually going to eat him (by the way, gross!), but this is too good an opportunity to miss. I may be small for a dinosaur, but I am the biggest beast he has ever encountered in the wild. He's all screaming and freaking out.

'**AAAAAAAAAHHHHHHHH!**' He jumps over the half wall and races down the road.

Daria shouts, 'Rory, stop! No eating friends. Remember?' Then, 'Oleg, it's just Rory.'

Oleg stops and smooths his hair like he totally wasn't just terrified. 'Rory?'

'Yup,' says Daria, who is loving being the bearer of all knowledge.

Oleg stares at me. 'Our Rory? Roary Rory? Why on earth is he dressed up as a ...?' Even Oleg is challenged here. 'An ostrich alligator mash-up? A gecko chicken? A velociraptor turkey? A ...'

'Deinonychus,' says Daria confidently.

'Day-in-what?' says Oleg.

'Deinonychus. They were what the velociraptors were based on in that movie. Only they liked the name velociraptor better.'

'Stole their look and gave them no credit. Not good,' says Oleg. 'That is an Unsubscribe from me. One-star review!'

Oleg then nearly chokes me to death, as he tries to wrestle off what he thinks is my fake head. I snap at him and he steps back.

'Take it easy, Rory,' he says. 'How does that mouth work? It's really well made. And those feathers feel like the real thing too. How is the tail attached? Is there a motor to move it like that?'

'He's not dressed up,' says Daria.

'But you just said he was? Like, what?'

'It's Rory. But he's not dressed up.'

I nod my huge head.

'OK, Oleg confused,' says Oleg.

'Daria explain,' says Daria.

This is how we talk sometimes. We silly.

Only now I can't talk so I just graagh as Daria tells Oleg what my mum told her.

'That is so cool,' says Oleg, staring at me. 'I only had beans on toast for dinner.'

I'm getting a bit uncomfortable with the Staring-at-Rory thing. I get that it is interesting and a bit unbelievable, but it is still Staring at Rory. Rory no likey.

Oleg says, 'Let's go to BuyMart and see if we can get some pie. I totally want to be a dinosaur too.'

Daria takes out her phone. 'Andy texted me back: "No Dino Pie on shelves. I asked

Manager. He laughed and walked away. Is this a joke Daria?"'

    'Weird,' says Oleg, looking at me.

    'Weird,' agrees Daria, looking at me.

LET'S SEE WHAT YOU CAN DO

'Well, if you are only a dinosaur until tomorrow, let's see what you can do,' says Oleg, starting to run.

'Chase us!' shouts Daria, laughing.

So, I do. It is much easier to move about out here than in the flat. It's the tail, the tail needs space.

Usually I'm fast, but today I'm Super Fast.

'Graagh!'

But after a while, even dinosaurs get tired. And bored.

If you've ever played chasing, you'll know that being the chaser is not as much fun as being chased. We try swapping after a bit, but I'm so much faster that they can't catch me anyway. We sit. The others have some questions.

Daria: 'Do you have super intense predator senses?'

Me: Nods.

Oleg: 'Do we look delicious?'

Me: Shakes head vigorously.

Daria: 'Can we look at your teeth?'

Me: Nods and opens wide.

Daria and Oleg: 'Wow, gross.' All pretend to faint dramatically.

Oleg, clutching his throat as if dying: 'No, the death breath ... Avenge me!'

Daria: 'Have you pooped yet?'

Me: Shakes head vigorously.

Daria and Oleg: Roll around laughing.

Oleg: 'Can you play *Big Battle World*?'

Me: Mimicking using the controls with my claws and totally smashing a boss.

Daria and Oleg: 'Okaaaaaaay.'

Oleg: 'You are really Roary Rory now. Get it? Like and Subscribe.'

Me: 'Graagh.'

Then Oleg shouts, 'Selfie time,' and we scrunch up together as Oleg takes selfies of us with Daria's phone.

'Look fierce,' says Oleg, and I do.

Oleg with a really terrified face, hand to his chest in fear. **CLICK**.

Me with my mouth open and Oleg with his head in my mouth. **CLICK**.

Me with my wing-arms around Daria and Oleg and those two giving a thumbs-up sign. **CLICK**.

Then Mum is shouting from her bedroom window that it's time to come in.

This has been an interesting experience. I'll be glad to be a kid in the morning, even though it would have been kind of awesome to see One-Two's reaction to dino-mode me. I give a claw wave to the gang.

'Glad we dino-saw you!' says Oleg with a thumbs-up.

I am definitely not Liking and Subscribing.

I'M NOT GOING TO TALK ABOUT IT

Mum has cleaned up all the smashed plates and stuff (from my earlier tail-swishing) and has one earbud in while she chats with a friend. She waves me towards the bathroom. I go in and attempt to pick up my toothbrush. This is not going to work.

I look at the toilet. I look at my tail. This is not going to work either. You probably don't want too much detail about this – and even if you do, this is not one of those things that I am willing to share. I'll just say, it involves the shower and a bucket and more help from Mum than I am totally comfortable with. But, better out than in.

I will totally be glad to not have to do that again.

I am feeling really tired now. It must be the dinosaur stuff wearing off. I nearly go to get my pyjamas, then I remember that I am not that shape. I don't feel cold anyway.

Mum has tidied up my room a bit. I'm not always OK with that but today I am. I need the extra space.

'Sweetie, it might be a bit of a squash in your bed, but I think you'll just about fit,' Mum says from the doorway.

I jump onto my bed, trying not to trash my duvet with the claws. I go to lie down, but that doesn't seem a natural position for this body. I come off the bed and try the corner between my desk and the window. Mum brings my duvet and a few blankets for me to sit on. I tuck my tail around me, my feet under me, fold my wing-arms and rest my head on them. I think to myself that it's going to be weird to wake up in this position as a human in the morning.

NOT AN EMERGENCY

I wake up to see Mum freaking out at the same moment that I realise I am still a dinosaur.

Tail. Check.

Huge head. Check.

Feathers. Check.

No. No. No.

'It said it would wear off,' Mum says. 'What on earth are we going to do now?'

I don't know, but I hope Mum can figure something out quickly. I am not staying like this.

Mum starts pacing around, rubbing her hands through her hair. 'I don't care what the label says about not seeking medical help. I'm ringing the clinic.'

She walks in circles with her phone for a bit, then puts it down on the counter. 'I'll try them again at nine.'

It is only 6:45AM.

She starts to get out the breakfast stuff. I can tell she is stressed because she is biting her lip.

'Will you have Oaty Krunch?' she asks.

I shake my head.

'Oh, right. Carnivore. I have eggs. What about scrambled eggs?'

I shake my head.

'Boiled eggs?'

I shake my head.

'Poached eggs?'

I shake my head. Does she think I'm an oviraptor?

'I have BuyMart sausages here. I was going to cook them tonight,' she says, looking in the fridge. 'Will you have them now?

I nod vigorously. I can't help it but I also gnash and drool.

She gives me an odd look. 'You may be a dinosaur, but I'm not feeding my kid raw sausages, so just wait for a few minutes.'

As she cooks them the smell is so amazing that I have to stop myself running around the flat. There is not really space for the tail around here so I would totally cause havoc by doing my normal up-and-down the corridor run. I flap instead.

The sausages are delicious. The best sausages I have ever eaten.

As I don't have to get ready for school or worry about clothes and shoes, I think I'll see how good dinosaurs' reactions are on *Big Battle World*. Mwah-ha-ha. Dino-Rory is going to kick some boss butt!

I graagh for Mum's attention and nod towards my computer.

'Do you want to try and play?' asks Mum.

I nod.

'OK, I suppose so,' she says.

I crouch in front of it. Mum shoves the

screen back a bit because my head is so huge. I press the power button with a claw. The home screen comes on. It looks weird, all pixelly. My eyesight is too good now. It's hard to read words and to scan. I need to move my head a lot. Tilting my head kind of works.

Big Battle World loads fully and I just can't do it. I thought the controls would be the tricky bit, but I can't even look at the screen. It looks wrong and it gives me a headache.

The thoughts start to spin in my head and I feel a tightness in my chest.

'Graagh,' I shout.

'Oh, sweetie, is it not working out for you?' Mum asks.

I need to get to my room. My tail swishes and starts banging into stuff. I jump onto the kitchen table, then the counter, then down the short corridor to my room. Even turning around to kick the door closed is awkward and my tail hurts. My head hurts. And I don't want to break anything with this stupid body. I curl up in my corner and just stay there for ages with thoughts racing through my head.

After a while I can hear Mum on the phone.

'Hello, I need an emergency appointment. My son has turned into a dinosaur.'

'Yes, he is conscious.'

'No, he's not sleepy or unresponsive, but –'

'No, he's not running a temperature, but –'

'No, no injuries, but –'

'No, no rash, but –'

'Thursday? But that's two days away.'

'Yes, I understand.'

'Yes, I'm sure you're very busy.'

'Yes ... I see how he is not a critical case, but he's a dinosaur!'

'OK. See you Thursday at 10AM.'

Mum comes in, runs her hand through her hair and tucks a piece tightly behind her ear.

'Right, we are going to BuyMart to see what they are going to do about this,' she says.

HELLO, BIRDIE

This is like the time she marched me down to the school to let One-Two know that her son would never sneak in comics to rent out to other kids during 'boring' classes and that he should withdraw his accusations immediately. We almost got to the school gate that time before I confessed. After she had calmed down, I like to think she was just a tiny bit proud of my business sense.

Even in dino-mode I have trouble keeping pace with my mum when she is on a mission. Mum strides straight up to the tills in BuyMart.

'I want to see the manager,' she insists.

The guy with the big arms and the tiny beard hits the buzzer under the counter and continues scanning packets of frozen vegetables.

We wait and wait.

This is the time that my brain decides to register the fact that, although I am totally covered in feathers, I am actually naked. In the middle of BuyMart. With my mum. All I can do to deal with the stress is flap my wing-arms.

A small child with a snotty nose comes over and holds out a crisp packet towards me. 'Hello, birdie!'

I give a 'graagh', and they run back to their parent who gives me a super dirty look.

Eventually a guy with floppy hair and a slightly too big shirt, over slightly too small trousers, comes over to us. His name tag says:

Hi, I'm Shane

Manager

How can I help you?

Then he actually says, 'Hi, I'm Shane, Manager, how can I help you?'

Mum is fuming at this stage. I can see it in the gentle tapping of her foot and the folding of her arms. Shane doesn't seem to notice.

She points in my direction.

'This,' she says, 'happened to my son when he ate one of your pies.'

'Have you got the receipt?' Shane asks. He's not even looking at us; he's making hand signals at someone who is trying to stack pasta in aisle 3.

'No,' says Mum, 'but that's not the point.'

'No, what?' asks Shane, still distracted

71

by the now teetering pile of pasta in aisle 3.

'No, I don't have the receipt,' snaps Mum. 'But just look at him. You shouldn't be selling food that turns kids into dinosaurs.'

'Do you have the item to be returned?' asks Shane, as he sighs at the mess he is going to have to sort out in aisle 3.

'No, he ate it,' sighs Mum.

'I'm sorry. No item, no receipt, we can't refund,' says Shane, turning to walk away.

'I don't want a refund,' says Mum. 'I want my son to look like a kid again.'

Shane turns back with a smile. 'Please see our website for terms and conditions and our online customer service team will be delighted to answer any further enquiries. Have a great day.'

Then he leans over and whispers to my mum. 'I would be grateful if you would press the green button on our customer service survey on your way out.'

Then off he goes to deal with the pasta situation.

Mum is looking a bit stunned. People are weaving around us with their trolleys, sighing as we cause them to divert slightly.

'Let's go,' says Mum.

I wish I could be in human-mode right now so I can hold her hand. Just for a minute.

HE HAS
A NOTE

When we get home, Mum comes up with her worst plan ever. Two of her worst plans actually. She comes out of her bedroom with a few pairs of her huge comfy stay-at-home socks. They are mostly pink and fluffy and some have hearts on them. I buy her a pair for Christmas every year.

'You can't go to school with those huge claws exposed,' she says.

School? What? I look at her in what I hope is a questioning pose.

'Rory, I have work today. You're not sick, so you're just going to have to go to school.'

But, Mum, I want to say, *I'm a dinosaur.*

'If I don't go in, I won't get paid,' she says firmly. 'And we need to keep you in sausages. I'll write you a note.'

My mother believes all school problems can be solved by a good note.

'Can you carry your school bag in your jaws?'

I nod. I mean, I suppose I can. If I have to.

Then she puts the fluffy socks on over my claws. I do not have the words to tell you how unimpressed I am by this.

Then my fun brain decides to pipe up, reminding me that now I am going to be naked in school! Naked, except for pink fluffy socks.

Great, thank you, brain! This is totally not turning out to be the best day of my life.

When you read books about kids turning into dinosaurs it is all about how great it is, how they get revenge on the bullies, defeat the bad guys and generally have fierce great fun. I wish this could be one of those books.

Even though so much has already happened today, it's not even eleven o'clock in the morning. Mum has had to ring work to organise being late in. I won't even miss all the morning classes. This seems unfair. I should at least get a day or two off. I mean, I'm a dinosaur now – how is life just going on like normal?

I arrive at school just in time for the end of small break. Daria spots me and runs over.

'Nice socks,' she says.

We try to sneak into the building unnoticed, but One-Two is waiting at the door. He looks me up and down in bewildered disapproval. (This is his default setting.)

'Rory, take that costume off immediately. This is not a theatre.'

How does he know it's me? I try to explain but what comes out is, 'Graagh, gnash, gnash, graagh.'

I really have not got the hang of this body. One-Two is starting to go red in the face.

'RORY, WHAT DID YOU JUST SAY? YOU WILL NOT USE THAT KIND OF LANGUAGE HERE.'

At that moment Daria says the magic words. 'He has a note, sir.'

THE PRINCIPAL'S OFFICE

'Right, to the principal's office. Both of you!' says One-Two, turning and striding back to his classroom.

To be honest, I am relieved not to be following him as we turn left down the corridor.

We wait outside the green door. The new shiny sign says *Ms O'Leary*, but we all call her Trudi. She insists. Oleg says Trudi is a dog's name. Mum says Trudi is a person's name and we shouldn't joke about names and the woman is just trying to connect with us, and not to be paying too much attention to Oleg because his humour isn't always kind.

'Come in, come in,' says Trudi. 'What have you two been up to now?'

She peers at me closely. 'Oh, I see. Rory, I love the costume, but it's not appropriate for the school environment. You'll be a distraction in class and we can't be having distractions in class, can we, children?'

We both shake our heads.

'He has a note,' says Daria.

I'm glad it's Daria with me.

Ms O'Leary reads the note.

Dear Ms O'Leary,
Rory will be a dinosaur for the next few days, until we can get a doctor's appointment.
This is not his fault.
Sincerely,

'Well, well, this is very unusual. Very unusual indeed,' Trudi mutters to herself.

She looks at me. 'How are you feeling, Rory?'

I shrug and look at Daria. She goes into spokesperson mode.

'He's fine, miss. But he can't talk,' she says. Then she adds, 'Well, not human anyway, but he can understand us.'

I am not sure that I actually am fine but it's way too complicated to try and let them know.

'Call me Trudi, please. Teachers are people too, Daria,' Trudi says.

'Yes, miss,' Daria says. 'I mean, Trudi.'

Daria continues, 'I don't think he can use chairs, miss, and, like, I'm not quite sure what this has done to his brain.'

'Thank you, Daria,' says Trudi, before Daria can give her any more words of wisdom.

I don't appreciate the brain comment and will look forward to setting Daria straight on that one. I hadn't realised that Daria talks almost as much as me in human-mode. I suppose that's why we are friends. We don't get upset at talking over each other generally but it's a bit weird when only one of us can talk in words.

Trudi peers at me and says slowly, 'Do you understand me, Rory?'

I use the internationally agreed affirmative signal and nod. My bag swings about as I move my head and I notice the strap is now really drooly.

'Would you like to put the bag down, Rory?' asks Trudi.

I drop it gratefully and give my jaw a good wide stretch.

I then realise that Trudi and Daria are staring at me in fascination (Daria) and horror (Trudi).

'Those are remarkable teeth, Rory,' Trudi says. 'Quite remarkable.'

'He's not allowed to eat humans,' says Daria.

I think to myself that there is no need for her to mention this, but then I notice a flicker of relief cross Trudi's face.

'Right,' says Trudi, standing up and

straightening her skirt. 'Well, we do try to be as inclusive as we can. You two wait here and I'll talk to Mr Buckley about classroom accommodations for a ...' She pauses. 'A dinosaur student? Or a student who is currently a dinosaur? Which is your preference, Rory?'

I shrug.

FAN CLUB

One-Two is not happy, but I get to sit at the back of the class on the floor. I don't have to go to the whiteboard or answer aloud. In fact, I don't think I'm allowed to answer at all. He still wants written work, but I'm not sure how I'll manage that. I can kind of hold a pencil in my mouth, although I keep gnashing through it accidentally and the page ends up covered in drool.

Everyone in the back row is grossed out by my breath, so they keep moving forward, and now most of the class is squashed up by the front. It means loads of space for me but it's kind of lonely back here.

At last, it's lunch break. Mum has packed salami and chicken slices for my lunch. For some reason I go into a bit of a frenzy while eating, and end up with everyone backing away slowly. Mum popped in some juice too but I burst it before I can drink it. There is a water fountain at our school, but I can't quite manage to manoeuvre my big long head into it.

I'm thinking too human. What does dino-mode me need to do? Aha! With a bit of flapping and a jump I perch on top of the water fountain and can just manage to manoeuvre myself down to drink with my huge tail balancing me.

Loads of kids stop to stare, so I give them a 'graagh' and a gnash of my jaws, but most just think that is awesome and want me to do it again. There are about twelve small kids who have started following me around. I catch one of them pulling out a tail feather and running back to his co-conspirators. It hurt too. The more I gnash at them the happier they seem to be, so I'm now ignoring them in the hope that they will get bored and find something more interesting to do at school than follow a dinosaur around all day.

When I go out to the yard more kids want me to chase them, which I do for a bit but then I get tired. I see Daria, Oleg and

a couple of other kids at our spot, chatting away excitedly. I walk over, stand next to them and dino-wave at everyone. They stop talking. Why do I feel awkward?

'We were talking about the Doom Boss,' says Daria after a weird silence.

'About how we are doomed to never beat him,' says Oleg. Then, with a thumbs-up: 'Like and Subscribe, people, Like and Subscribe to the Oleg.'

There is a general sigh.

'We have your dino-reflexes now,' says Daria looking at me.

I shake my big head.

'Can you not play?' she asks.

I shake my big head.

Oleg puts a hand on my shoulder. 'That is terrible news, my feathered friend, terrible.'

I just kick at the ground with my useless claws in my ridiculous socks.

We kind of all just stand there awkwardly for a bit and then thankfully the bell rings.

The day doesn't get better. Memorable events include: smashing a toilet seat (accidentally), my breath making the class hamster faint, breaking seventeen pencils (accidentally), my soggy written work sending One-Two apoplectic, Trudi coming in and escorting One-Two from the classroom, us having a substitute teacher for the afternoon, Trudi calling my mum and suggesting that I take a few sick days until 'the situation' is remedied. Worst of all, me overhearing Daria and Oleg planning to play *Big Battle World* later. And I had thought school days couldn't get any worse.

No Cheese

So, I'm off school for a few days. Today, Mum has work, and Lucy next door has put her back out so she can't watch me. I get Lex.

Lex has been our neighbour for ever. Lex used to have another name, but he changed it when we started calling him 'he'. We don't use his other name any more. That would be rude and insulting and cause Lex pain. He was always one of the quieter big kids, even before he became a goth. Although he hangs out with his friends in dark stairwells dressed in black and looking all broody, he watches anime with me and makes the best peanut-butter sandwiches. I think he's about seventeen or eighteen but it's hard to tell. When I ask him, he says that information is classified. Not big on chat, our Lex.

Mum leaves money for Lex to pop to the shop before lunch and get us some food because I have eaten every meat product in the fridge for breakfast and I even tried some cheese. That was not a good plan.

Note: Cheese is not recommended for dinosaurs. It just gets jammed up between the teeth and a washing-up brush is required to remove it.

Note to Note: I recommend thoroughly washing all washing-up liquid from brush before using in dinosaur's mouth.

Note to Note to Note: It is advisable to keep hands clear when removing cheese from mouth as dinosaur cannot always control his bite reflex.

First, we try to watch some anime. There is a new series of *Hawke Hill* and we plan to watch it all. This would normally be amazing, but I'm finding it a bit weird watching TV. Like with the computer it is tricky to watch and hurts my head. Also, in dino-mode I startle quite easily and lots of the action on the screen sends me into hyper-alert hunting mode. Which makes it difficult to stay still and concentrate on the show.

It is even tricky to get comfortable on the couch. I can kind of perch on the back, but I need Lex's body weight on the seat. When Lex forgets that and stands up to get something, the couch and I tumble backwards with a huge thump and graagh. Jebey bangs on his ceiling/our floor to let us know that we need to quiet down.

Eventually Lex suggests we go to BuyMart. I don't think Mum meant for me

to go too, but I can't say that to Lex. I really need a change of scenery anyway and my stomach is starting to rumble. I want food. A lot of food. Actually, I want sausages. BuyMart sausages. This carnivore body needs feeding.

So, off we go, Lex and I. Me in my feathered dinosaur-ness, him in his black gothiness. We are a weird pairing, even for a Wednesday morning in BuyMart.

SAUSAGES

We load up our shopping basket with sausages. Well, Lex does, and I skulk nearby keeping an eye out for Shane, Manager, but he doesn't seem to be around today.

As we are checking out, I notice that two tills over is a woman with a trolley full of sausages and she is staring at us whenever she thinks we are not looking. There is also a man further back in that queue with a basket full of sausages. I nudge Lex and try to subtly draw his attention to them.

Subtle doesn't really work with Lex. Eventually Lex notices my nudges, though I practically have to bruise a rib first. It is so frustrating not being able to talk when I want to. I nod towards the people with the sausages.

He gives me a questioning look.

I nod towards the other people's sausages again and then pointedly at ours.

'Do you think there are others?' he asks.

I nod. Yes, I hope there are others. Maybe all over Cork City kids have been eating dinosaur pie. Thank you, brain, for a hopeful thought at last.

We need to make a decision on whether or not to follow the other sausage people

home. My mum always goes on about how raw meat must be kept in the fridge or it will go bad so I think it's better to take the sausages home first and come back later to check out other suspicious sausage purchasers. Also, I am hungry and I cannot focus on anything else.

This makes it sound like Lex and I had a huge discussion.

It was actually like this:

Lex: 'Home?'

Me: Nod.

By the time we get home I am a ravenous beast. Lex cooks up the sausages. I can cook for myself in my human form but as a dinosaur I am a disaster. It's the claws and the lack of opposable thumbs. Lex takes his time. Lex takes his time about everything. Lex is super chilled, even with a drooling dinosaur hopping from foot to foot and gnashing behind him. He is like the opposite of me sometimes.

I have always liked sausages. They were never my favourite food or anything, but once or twice a week, yum. But now, I love sausages. I crave them. They are the best thing. I did not realise before just how amazing sausages are. How could other foods even begin to compare?

There are only sausages.

Sausages are totally the best.

Lex lifts the sausages onto a plate and I give him a head-to-one-side look.

He seems to get it and just tips all the sausages onto the table, then turns his back as I messily devour them.

Now that I have eaten, I can turn my attention to the hunt.

WE ARE TERRIBLE AT THIS

We are back outside BuyMart to chase down other sausage-buying people. I mean, to observe and follow the sausage purchasers.

BuyMart is on the edge of town, over the bridge and right at the roundabout. Everyone calls it the BuyMart roundabout. We lurk around the trolleys for a bit, trying to look inconspicuous, then decide to sit on the low wall that surrounds the car park. We can see the door from here.

We totally don't look suspicious. Not. Especially playing Rock, Paper, Scissors. Luckily, Andy the security guard (Daria's brother) is around the back by the bins having a chat with the woman who calls everyone 'Love'.

It soon becomes apparent we are terrible at this. There is no way we can spot the sausage purchasers from outside the shop as all the sausages are in bags by the time they get near us.

Lex comes up with a plan that involves us making the most out of the remaining €4.70 we find in our pockets. Well, in Lex's pockets. For obvious reasons, I don't have pockets. We will go in and buy one item at a time and join the longest queue so we can scope for sausages. Before we can implement the Sausage Plan, I catch a scent.

I graagh at Lex and point to a woman with purple hair, who is carrying two heavy bags.

'Sausages?' Lex looks at me with one raised goth-brow. (Like a normal eyebrow, but he has rubbed something black into it.)

I nod. My dino nose is good for something.

'Want to follow?' asks Lex.

I nod my head.

Our following skills are nearly as good as our inconspicuous-lurking skills, but thankfully she is too preoccupied to notice us.

We end up at Bracken Court, a circle of duplexes with a green in the centre. Purple-Haired Woman climbs the outside stairs of number 42. As she puts the bags down to fumble for her keys, I try to get into a good position to look as the door opens.

But – nothing.

The door closes.

What now?

Lex is leaning against a tree on the green, which is a good plan as it has just started to drizzle. You know, that damp light rain that looks all innocent and nearly dry but slowly seeps into your bones? I stand next to him. He's muttering to himself.

I look at him quizzically.

He goes a very ungothish pink.

'Talking to the tree,' he mumbles.

OK, I think, *let's just go along with this.* I give what I hope is a look that means, 'How interesting, that is totally not a weird thing to be doing.'

'Oak,' he says. 'The oldest being around here.'

I do a dino nod with my dino take on a serious expression of respect. This seems to be the correct response, as Lex twitches his mouth in what I suspect may have been the tiniest of smiles. But maybe I am imagining it.

I'm finding the lack of movement frustrating. No disrespect to Lex, but he is practically a tree himself. I start to pace around the green but keep my beady dino eyes on number 42. I am about to suggest we go back to the supermarket when there is movement from an upstairs window. These dino senses are so sharp!

It is just a quick flick of a curtain. For a moment I see a small face. A small reptilian face. A small dinosaur face. For the briefest of seconds our eyes meet, then they are gone.

HERD INSTINCT

My heart is beating so fast and strong that it must be visible through my chest. There are other dinos! It isn't just me! There is a pulling feeling in my stomach. I have to meet this other dinosaur. This is stronger even than the urge for sausages. Is this herd instinct? Were Deinonychus even herd animals? (Another question for Daria.)

Or is it just relief at not being the only one?

Lex, Lex, I saw them. There's a dinosaur in number 42, I want to shout. Instead, I butt him in the arm and motion with my head towards the house.

'You can't just call in, wee guy. You might terrify them.'

I totally ignore him and run towards the steps, my tail swishing, my wing-arms flapping. Up the steps I go, and then I head-butt the door gently a few times. It's the best way I can think of knocking. I can hear hurried and hushed conversation and the sounds of someone approaching. I can smell sausages and another scent that seems familiar.

The door opens – it's Purple-Haired Woman, looking a bit frazzled. She stares at the big dinosaur head on me, but thankfully doesn't scream. She just sighs and ushers me inside.

'I thought you would never work up the courage to call in,' she says. 'You were going to wear a path on that green, pacing up and down. You might as well invite in yer man lurking by the tree too. I don't imagine you can talk.'

I nod and stick my head out and gesture over at Lex. He is totally in his own world. His little Lex bubble of thought. Eventually I let out a loud graagh. Lex jumps up, checks no one else is watching and strolls over towards us. Hands in his pockets, head down, as if he is not really being summoned by a dinosaur.

As he arrives at the door, I am nearly knocked over by a small dinosaur, about half my height, banging enthusiastically into me. Not aggressively. More like a friendly puppy attack.

KEEP UP THE GOOD WORK!

Purple-Haired Woman closes the door and waves us into the sitting room. The very excited small dinosaur runs ahead. Lex has gone shy and is trying to melt into the wall.

'Come, sit down here.' The woman pats the couch she is now sitting on, and Lex, eyes to the ground, sits on it, jammed up against the far end. He has a big need for personal space, our Lex.

I stand by the fireplace opposite the couch. Their room is bigger than our sitting room and is filled with toy boxes, and there are pictures stuck on the walls, mostly drawings of fire engines and police trucks. There is a mini trampoline in the corner of the room.

The small dinosaur, I notice, has bunny slippers taped on, and is bouncing rapidly up and down on the trampoline while gnashing and gnaaring.

'Well, hi,' says the woman. ' I'm Laura and this is Tina. She's four. In human years.'

I graagh.

Lex grunts.

Awkward silence descends.

Silence makes me jumpy. I'm not good with silences. Usually, I just keep talking. Rory no likey not being able to talk.

Laura jumps up and starts rooting around in a toy box.

'Let's try this.'

She takes out a pink sparkly laptop, fiddles around with it a bit, then hands it to me. It's a toddler's toy, with one of those tiny grey screens.

I type with a claw as Laura looks at the screen. 'Hi, I'm Rory and that's Lex.'

Then we both jump as the computer says, '**GOOD JOB!**'

'Sorry about that,' says Laura, laughing, 'but nice to meet you, Rory and Lex. Did you have dinosaur pie for dinner too?

I nod.

Lex says hi and goes back to typing away on his phone.

'I don't want to be a dinosaur,' I type.

'**THAT'S AWESOME!**' blares the laptop.

Laura nods. 'Tina is enjoying it for now but I think she'd like things to be normal too. I've taken her to the doctor. They are totally flummoxed. They did some blood tests.'

'Graagh!' shouts Tina.

Laura looks at Tina and nods.

'Tina did not like the blood tests,' sighs Laura. 'She bit the nurse.'

'Graagh, graagh,' agrees Tina, who is still jumping up and down.

The trampoline is making those annoying squeaky sounds. It is her house, though, so I can't really ask her to stop. That kid has a lot of energy. I get that. Alex Danger Human Dynamo was a lot like that kid. Mum used to have to keep the door locked all the time or I'd be gone. I'd just run. I loved to run. Not to anywhere or really from anything but just for the running. Actually, I'd really love to run now.

'They are going to call us when they get the results of the tests,' says Laura. 'We hope it will wear off soon.'

'Me too,' I type.

'**SUPER WORK!**' says the computer.

'It will be fine,' says Laura. She pats me on the shoulder.

I'm not sure I believe her. She doesn't sound that confident.

'Can you give me your parents' phone number and I'll call them later? The more of us who get in contact with each other, the more power we have to get something done about this. BuyMart are now denying that they ever sold dinosaur pie.'

I type in Mum's name and number.

'**FANTASTIC!**' exclaims the laptop.

Laura nods towards Lex, whose thumbs are nearly a blur he is texting so fast. 'Will your brother take you home?'

'Not my brother,' I type. 'He's my responsible human.'

Lex gives a thumbs-up.

'**KEEP UP THE GOOD WORK!**' shouts the computer. It had to have the last word.

OPERATION MAKE RORY HUMAN AGAIN

Daria and Oleg call over after school.

'It's no fun without you in school,' says Oleg. 'Oleg so bored.'

'What about me?' says Daria. 'Aren't I fun?'

Oleg rolls his eyes, then nudges Daria. 'You Oleg friend. But Rory funny. Oleg miss Rory.'

'He's not dead,' says Daria.

Hello, I am actually right here, I want to say.

'But Oleg is right, school is way worse without you,' says Daria.

That is actually nice to hear.

Oleg jumps up. 'Pause, people. Did you hear that, Rory?'

I nod.

'What?' asks Daria.

'Ssh, let me savour the moment,' says Oleg.

I'm dino snort-laughing.

'What?' asks Daria again.

'You said, and I quote, "Oleg

is right,"' says Oleg. 'You know what this means?'

Daria rolls her eyes and hands her phone to Oleg.

'Selfie time!'

Daria is doing her bored face, Oleg giving a thumbs-up sign, my big dino head in the background. **CLICK**.

Then Daria opens her backpack. 'Rory, good news! Your bestest friend Daria has brought you a communication device.'

Great, I think, and my brain jumps to futuristic technology, automatic translators, brain-reading devices.

Out of her backpack she pulls a bright orange rectangular thing. It looks like a big chunky tablet but there is a clunky handle on the top and a plastic duck at the bottom of a long groove on one side.

There is a kind of screen, but it looks very dirty and scratched. I have no idea what it is but it is definitely designed for someone at least five years younger than me. The pink toy computer was far more technologically advanced.

I look at Daria quizzically.

'Rory, meet Ducky, your new communication device.'

Rory still no comprendo.

Then Daria unclips a pen with faded ducks printed on it from the bottom of the device and writes on the screen thing.

R O A R Y   R O R Y   R O A R S

'Can you read that easier than a computer or phone screen?' she asks.

I nod.

'It's a magnetic sketchpad,' she says. 'If you can't use phones with those claws of yours that means text-to-voice won't work, but I thought an old-school kid thing like this might work.'

It seems to be a day for old-school kids' toys. At least this one doesn't give me enthusiastic approval.

I stretch out a claw and try to scratch a word.

Daria slaps it away. 'No, Rory, it works with magnets. You need to use the pen.'

I shake my head. My experience of pencils at school does not bode well for the pen.

'Maybe not in your teeth,' says Oleg, who has now wrapped one leg behind his head and is hopping around on the other leg. He is double-jointed, super bendy, circus-level bendy. Elastic boy. Bendosaurus. Stretch Olegstrong, Olastic ... So many names. It keeps us amused for hours.

'Here,' says Daria, unwrapping a hair elastic from her ponytail and letting her hair fall down. She wraps the elastic around both my claw and the pen thingie.

Oleg unfolds his leg, jumps dramatically and points his two forefingers at Daria. 'Daria, folks. The brains of the operation.' Then he flops onto the couch.

I try the magnetic thingie.

'**OPERATION MAKE RORY HUMAN AGAIN?**' I write.

'Is that a thing?' asks Oleg.

I nod vigorously.

'You don't want to stay being a dinosaur?' Daria seems actually shocked.

I shake my head vigorously.

'OK, let's do the thing,' says Oleg. Then he adds. 'How exactly do we do the thing?'

We all stop to think.

At that moment Mum is heading out the door with the bag from our bin to put in the big bin downstairs.

'There's a bin at the back of BuyMart!' says Daria.

I start to flap as I guess where she's going with this.

'What, are you becoming a skip-diver now?' asks Oleg.

'No, silly,' says Daria.

'**CLUES**,' I write.

'And so, the intrepid explorers head off on another dangerous mission,' says Oleg in narrator voice. 'Will Rory remain a dinosaur for ever? Will Oleg always be this awesome? Will Daria ever stop giving Oleg the glare? Slowly fade to darkness. To be continued ...'

I head-butt Oleg. Gently.

CHIP-ROBBING THUGS

Andy, the security guard, is outside when we get to BuyMart. Daria has a plan to distract him while we hide behind some conveniently large people carriers.

'Hey, bro,' she says. 'Mum was wondering if you'd call her and let her know what's good on the special-offer shelf. She loves when you give her inside info.'

'They have just restocked it,' says Andy.

'Mum would be thrilled if you, like, messaged her now.'

'Fine,' says Andy, and off he wanders back in.

'Quick,' says Daria to us. 'Around the back now before Andy's brain catches up with him and he wonders why I can't just text Mum myself.'

We scoot around the back. The bin area is fenced off but the gate isn't locked. In we go.

Ew, the smell is disgusting. It's also totally overpowering and is seeping into every pore in my body. Do I still have pores? I suppose I do.

But smelling is one of my dino super-powers, so I try to focus and remember the smell of dinosaur pie so we don't have to go through all six giant bins. I point towards a huge green one in the corner. It is so full that the lid is pushed up in the air by badly tied rubbish bags which look like they are planning an escape.

There are gulls squawking and strolling around on the low roof behind the bin. They are tearing apart bags and tubs that they have grabbed from the half-open bin and are busily pecking at bits of stuff they have scavenged.

Well, they are mostly gulls. There is also one gull-sized, ridiculously cute Deinonychus that is sneaking up on its friends.

I graagh and point.

'I hate gulls,' says Oleg. 'Chip-robbing thugs. One-star review.'

Oleg obviously has unresolved gull issues.

'Graagh,' I say again, pointing at the tiny dino.

'Graagh,' the little thing says back as he turns around and catches sight of me. The gulls fly off to a higher piece of roof where they can glare at us in safety.

'No way! Tiny dino!' says Daria.

'Itty bitty widdle Wowy,' says Oleg helpfully.

I walk right up to the edge of the roof and the tiny dinosaur scampers over towards me. It then hops onto my wing-arm. The little thing looks up at me. 'Graagh?'

'Graagh,' I say gently back.

He gives a little burp.

'Let's call him Burp,' says Daria.

Oleg hears that as some kind of challenge and blasts out a huge burp himself.

We all look at him.

'What?' he says and laughs. 'Just saying hi to Burp.'

Burp seems happy walking up and down my back and wing-arms and tail, over my head and graaghing quietly to himself.

'Selfie time,' calls Oleg. Daria passes him the phone and pats him on the head sympathetically.

Me with Burp on my arm. **CLICK**.

Selfie of me, Daria and Oleg with Burp on Oleg's head. **CLICK**.

Selfie of us three just as Burp vomits on Oleg's hair. **CLICK**.

Daria grabs the phone while Oleg has a little freakout.

Close up of Oleg's hair, zoomed in on the vomited-up fluffy ball of ickiness. **CLICK**.

Then we get stuck into the super fun task of going through the bin. Well, Daria and I do. Oleg is dramatically gagging. So dramatically that I think he actually might really vomit.

'Gross, gross,' he keeps repeating.

It is not just Oleg's hair that's gross. The bin is not exactly smelling delicious and my super dino senses aren't making this easier.

Burp is helping by perching on my back.

'Look there,' says Daria at the exact time

that I spot it too. A black bag that has been torn open by the gulls. I can see a few pie tubs with 'Dinosaur Pie' written on them.

'We have evidence,' says Daria.

'Yes!' says Oleg, punching the air, distracted from his freaking out at last.

We both look at him.

'You can't eat it,' says Daria.

'But Oleg want to be dino,' says Oleg.

I whack him on the arm.

'Dirty,' says Daria, waving a finger at him. 'Oleg no eaty.'

Oleg laughs and shrugs. 'Too gross anyway and why would I want to change these stunning good looks? My fortune, people, my fortune,' he says, pointing to his own face.

I wish I could roll these eyes. Daria does a good enough job for the two of us.

We are so distracted we don't hear anyone enter the bin area until there is a cough. The kind of cough designed to let you know you have been caught red-handed. It's a cough One-Two would be proud of.

We all stop and turn. It is Shane, Manager.

'This is private property,' he says, hands on his hips.

UNSUBSCRIBE!

In my panic my brain gets overridden by some kind of dino instinct, because I find myself just running straight at Shane, Manager. Wings flapping. Graaghing loudly. In the background I hear Oleg shout 'Get the Blethers!' as he and Daria charge after me.

Shane turns and runs away from us around the building towards the main entrance, shouting 'Andy!' at the top of his voice.

I just spy Andy, appearing out the door, with his phone to his ear, as we jump over the low wall. Luckily there is a gap in the traffic and we cross the road and head

for the bridge, hoping to get over it and disappear in the estates quicker than Andy can figure out what is going on.

But both Shane and Andy are running now. We pass the goth gang skulking along the bridge railings, looking all edgy. They don't even register us going past until I graagh and Lex turns towards me. He gives a small nod of his head, but we are gone.

Daria and Oleg are so slow. *C'mon, c'mon.*

I glance behind, Shane and Andy are across the road and coming over the bridge.

Then suddenly they aren't, because I see Lex stick out a big boot and Shane trip over it. Andy stops to help and we are gone.

Thank you, Lex, I think, as we scoot around the corner, cross the road, then up behind number 15 and into the scrub, opposite the school.

We are hidden here, in the trees. Just us and an empty crisp packet and a couple of squashed cans. Although a small robin is shouting at us that it is actually he who owns here. He is staying a safe distance from us, though.

I catch my breath, and the other two do the same. Well, actually the other three, as Burp still has a firm grip on my back.

Oleg hasn't forgiven him for the vomiting incident. 'Unsubscribe,' he says pointing at the little guy. 'One-star review!' Harsh words from Oleg.

I notice Daria is clutching a black sack. I hadn't registered it in all the drama. She did it: she thought to bring the evidence with her. Trust Daria to keep a cool head and remember what's important.

We stay in the bushes for a bit, long

enough to plan a route home that goes nowhere near BuyMart. Burp hops onto my tail and I have a sniff before we leave the cover of the trees to make sure the coast is clear.

A FIRST FOR HUMANITY

We go back to my flat. Oleg wants to wash his hair here because his mum will freak if he arrives home with goo-hair.

So after we introduce Burp to Mum, Daria does the explaining about the rest of the stuff. I should take lessons from her. Me explaining usually ends up in trouble and a lot of confusion. Daria explaining usually ends up in the adults bending to her will. It is some kind of weird superpower she has.

Daria: 'So, Rebecca, we were round BuyMart and saw this bin there, totally open, and there was a bag sticking out, and Rory smelt something, with his dino senses, like, and it turned out this bag had that dinosaur pie stuff in it, so we thought it might be evidence, like, and – well, here it is. Maybe it will help Rory be Rory again.'

Mum: 'OK, well, thanks. And yuck. I'm not sure what to do with this. Let's just bag it up a few more times and leave it by the door. We could maybe take it to the garda station in the morning, see what they think about it.'

Mum pulls out a roll of black sacks and pulls on some rubber gloves. She shoos Daria off to scrub her hands, so Daria joins Oleg, who is still trying to wash his head with the shower while keeping the rest of him dry. He keeps muttering 'Oleg not happy' and 'Gross.'

Mum has a quick look in the bag and pulls out some pages with typing on them.

'Graagh?' I ask.

'Mmm, memos,' she says. 'Interesting.' Then she stuffs them in a separate bag before putting them back in. She triple bags the lot, sprays everything with some floral room freshener, then apologises as I freak out over the smell.

'Sorry, Rory, it's just ewww, and I'm not feeling the best anyway.' She must be able to read my concerned dino face because she adds, 'Just a bit of a cold and a cough.'

In all my worrying about being a dinosaur I hadn't even noticed Mum was sick.

Daria and Oleg emerge from the bathroom, Oleg looking very unimpressed and Daria explaining how lucky he is.

'Like, you are probably the first human ever to be vomited on by a dinosaur. We have never coexisted before. Like, this is a first for humanity, Oleg.'

Oleg brightens up. 'Really? Did you get it on video?'

'No, Oleg, I didn't. But there are photos.'

'Mm, maybe we could get him to do it again.'

'Not right now, you won't,' says Mum, nodding towards the culprit, who is curled up fast asleep on a hoodie of mine on the armchair.

I hope he doesn't poop in that hoodie. It's one of my favourites.

We all kind of jump when there is a really loud knock on our door.

No Fair

Mum shoos me out of sight and answers the door. It's Shane, Manager, from BuyMart, all hands on his hips and posing. Andy is trying to disappear behind him.

'Have you come about Rory?' asks Mum. 'Have you found a cure?'

'Rory?' asks Shane, looking confused for a moment. Then he shakes his head. 'I am here on official BuyMart business. Property has been stolen from BuyMart premises and I want it returned immediately. It is the sole property of BuyMart and you have no authority to be possessing it.' He is going a bit purple in the face from all the suppressed rage.

Mum is looking at him quizzically. Like he's a fish who has started talking.

'Give back the rubbish the kids stole from the skip,' he says.

Andy mutters, 'He was going to call the gardaí but I told him there was no need to get them involved. I told him that I happened to know where these kids lived, even though they are Total Strangers To Me.' He looks meaningfully at Daria, who was about to protest, but who now decides to disappear back into the bathroom.

After Shane and Andy leave with the bag, we are all unusually silent. Horribly silent. Miserably silent. The worst silence ever! Even the tiny snores coming from Burp, the weird little dino bird, can't cheer me up now.

'No fair,' says Oleg.

'No fair,' agrees Daria.

'Graagh,' I say.

'No fair indeed,' says Mum.

'All of that for nothing,' says Daria.

'Unsubscribe to today,' says Oleg.

'I agree, Oleg, I agree,' says Mum, as she puts the kettle on.

After Daria and Oleg go home, Mum carefully picks up Burp, still asleep in the hoodie, and brings him to my room.

'It will be OK, Rory,' she says. 'We'll get through this, we always do. We have that doctor's appointment in the morning. They'll have a solution.'

But I know it won't be OK. Laura has already brought Tina to the doctor and there is no solution. This is my awful life for *ever*.

Mum goes to sleep early and it's really late now, but I still can't sleep. There is so much weirdness to process and the late-night worries catch up on me. I hate those late-night worries.

My late-night worries are usually about getting in trouble at school or wondering if Mum is OK.

Tonight, I'm wondering if I will ever be a kid again. Will my friends think I'm too weird to hang out with after a while? Will I be able to play *Big Battle World* ever again? I miss my hands and all the stuff I can do with them. I miss talking. I miss gaming. I miss talking about gaming. I even miss brushing my teeth. I just want to be in my own body again, to be Roary Rory. Like, I know I'm still me but I'm also not me. Do you know what I mean?

I can hear Mum coughing in her sleep, so Burp and I sneak quietly into her room and curl up on her floor. I feel safer in here where I can hear her noises.

BURP ALARM

I'm awake early next morning. It might be because there is a tiny dinosaur climbing over me and pouncing on my tail. Burp is the best alarm clock. If he stays, I'll never be late for school again. But if he stays it would be because he is still a dino, and if he is still a dino, I would be still a dino. Would I even be able to go back to school? Not that I miss school or anything. I miss my life, though. It was kind of ordinary, and tricky sometimes, but it was my life. I'm sure Burp misses being a gull too and hanging out with his gull buddies.

Burp wakes Mum and we all get up and go to the kitchen. Mum pours some cough syrup into the little plastic cup that comes with it.

'That will remind me to take it with food,' she says.

She's busy heating up the pan for my sausages. I'm perched on a stool and dangling a string for Burp to attack. He is full of mischief this morning. When he's had enough string attacking, he jumps onto the ledge, and before I can stop him, he is lapping up Mum's medicine.

'Graagh!' I shout. The little cup falls over, spilling the pink goo all over the countertop.

Mum turns around and realises what is happening. 'No, Burp!'

He has managed to get a few licks in before we bat him away.

'Graagh?' I ask Mum.

'He'll be OK,' says Mum. 'It's only over-the-counter stuff and he just got a tiny bit. It probably isn't even helping my cough it's so mild.'

She stretches out and rubs Burp. 'He's such a cute little thing,' she says.

Burp snaps his tiny but fierce teeth and Mum pulls her hand back quickly.

'Feisty too,' says Mum. 'Right, let's get you two some sausages for breakfast.'

By the time breakfast is ready, Burp has vanished. He is not curled up asleep anywhere.

'Graaagh!' I say to Mum.

'Well, he must be somewhere,' says Mum. 'He can hardly get out of the flat.'

Oh no! He couldn't have, could he?

I run to Mum's room and, just like I was afraid of, the top window is open.

Poor Burp didn't have Daria to tell him that his feathers aren't flight feathers.

WAIT, WHAT?

I let out a roar – not an actual roar, obviously, but a graagh roar – and Mum comes running in. I point to the window.

'Oh no,' whispers Mum.

I am shaking. I can't look. Mum walks quickly to the window, takes a deep breath and leans out to peer down.

I am flapping and my chest is tight, so tight, and my legs want to run.

Mum turns around and says, 'Not there.'

Just as I am breathing out there is a knock on the door.

Mum closes the window firmly first, then gets the door.

It's Jebey, from downstairs, holding Burp, who is wriggling to get down.

'I was sitting on my chair outside my window, reading my paper, and this little gecko or whatever landed, flump, on my head. I think to myself that he has something to do with Rory upstairs.'

I run over and Burp climbs onto my back.

'Thanks, Jebey, it won't happen again,' says Mum, about to close the door, when Jebey clears his throat.

'I've been meaning to ask, Rebecca. I don't want to be rude,' says Jebey, head down and kicking his feet about like a nervous kid. 'I noticed that recently Rory looks different from other kids and I thought maybe it was aliens. And I wonder if you could introduce me? To your leader?'

Mum stares blankly at Jebey for a few minutes. Burp has disappeared again, but at least I know the window is closed now.

'Jebey,' says Mum gently, 'we haven't met aliens. We aren't aliens. Rory looks like this as the result of a food-poisoning incident.'

Jebey sighs and turns to walk away.

Mum shouts after him: 'If we ever do meet aliens, Jebey, you'll be the first to know.'

She turns to me and shrugs. Then she runs towards the stove, just as I register the burning smell.

Twenty minutes later, the second batch of sausages is cooked. The apartment is quite smokey, though, as the extractor fan is rubbish and we can't open the windows because ... Burp.

Burp doesn't come out for sausages, which is weird. After I wolf mine down, I start to look for our hiding expert again. Eventually I find him under the desk in my room, curled up, deep in a pile of clothes that are possibly dirty, or maybe were clean but have been on the floor so long they crossed over to the dark side and are dirty again.

He is pretty cute, but ... *what the heck?*

Loads of his feathers have fallen out and as I look at him his head and teeth seem to be shrinking. He is making tiny little moaning noises in his sleep. Did he get injured in the fall?

'Graagh!' I call Mum.

'What now?' she asks when she arrives, in what I call her exasperated voice. Well, I can't blame her for being a bit stressed. I suppose it's not your typical morning and we were never good at mornings anyway.

I point at Burp. He appears to be getting furrier. Ginger fur is sprouting where the feathers have fallen out. His tail is shrinking. Getting thinner and furrier.

Rory confused. Rory very confused. And frightened. Rory bit frightened too.

Is Burp's dino pie wearing off? But why isn't he turning back into a gull?

'Rory, are you sure he's a gull?' asks Mum, echoing my thoughts. She does that sometimes.

I nod, but then I think. There was a flock of gulls and Burp was chasing them – we just presumed he was a gull. Hmm. His vomit was very like a fur ball.

I begin to frantically shake my head. Then I see the orange magnetic sketchpad thingie on my desk and whack it a few times until Mum gets the message and ties the pen to my claw.

I write out a word.

C A T

Burp is a cat.

I watch, fascinated, as Burp continues to transform. Mum goes for her shower, as we have that doctor's appointment in a bit and she doesn't want to be late.

Soon there is just a sleeping cat, bigger than a kitten but not quite fully grown, and a pile of feathers. He wakes up, has a huge

stretch and yawn, and winds himself around my feet in that catty way of asking for food.

C'mon, Burp, I think, and we go to the kitchen, where I flick him the sausages we had kept for him.

'Your turn,' says Mum, as she comes out of the bathroom.

I give her a questioning look.

'You need a shower, love. You don't smell really great. Very dinosaury.'

Rory insulted.

But Mum is probably right. I haven't showered since what I think of as BT (before transformation). I don't seem to sweat but I probably have a bit of a dino funk going on. And my claws could do with a scrub. Got to be clean for Dr Shanahan. She disapproves of dirty children and presumably dirty dinosaurs too.

EXPECTING THE WORST

When we arrive at the doctor's office, we have to wait to talk to Sheri on reception. She is on the phone and admiring her own nails. Sheri is Daria's aunt and she knows everything about everybody and Mum always says, 'Tell her nothing.'

Eventually Sheri hangs up the phone and makes eye contact with Mum. 'Hello, Rebecca. How's things?'

Mum glances over at me. Sheri doesn't look surprised. 'Hello, Rory,' she says as if I'm not a dinosaur at all.

'Take a seat,' she says. 'Dr Shanahan will be ready for you shortly.'

We usually have to wait ages in the waiting room, but not today. Which is good, as the woman in the corner is clutching her huge handbag very tightly and giving me dagger looks.

Dr Shanahan is about two hundred years old and likes to peer down her glasses at children. Even though I'm tall now, I still get the feeling I did when I was little. Like she is seeing into my soul and is not all that impressed. She is the one person that makes me speechless.

She swings around her giant swivel chair to face us, and waves at Mum to sit on one of the two rickety patient chairs. For obvious reasons, I can't, so I kind of try to melt into the wall. I am terrified she will send me away to a secret military base where they will do experiments on me and I will never see my mum again. If I was human now, I would be fighting back the tears, but I don't seem to be able to dino-cry. Sheri probably set off some alarm the minute she caught sight of me and there are armed dudes with stun guns and a cage on their way. My life is over. Should I just go on a rampage to tear myself free and go live in the woods terrorising passersby?

Dr Shanahan does the over-the-glasses thing and looks at Mum.

Mum appears to have lost the power of speech and just points to me and manages one word: 'Rory.'

'I see,' says Dr Shanahan. 'And how long has he been like this?'

'Since Monday.'

'And why on earth did you not bring him in on Monday?' She lowers her glasses so much that they're about to fall off their perch.

'I called,' says Mum. 'But this was the first available appointment.'

The glasses get shoved back up, and Dr Shanahan types something on her computer with her two forefingers. Then she peers at the screen.

'Very rare, normally.' She nods at me. 'But this is the twelfth case I've seen this week. Perfectly healthy children turned into some sort of giant bird creature.'

'Deinonychus,' says Mum.

'Pardon?'

'Apparently he's a Deinonychus.'

A questioning look from Dr Shanahan.

'It's the type of dinosaur he is.'

'I see,' says Dr Shanahan, turning back to her computer. 'Deinonychus indeed. Did he consume a food product labelled "Dinosaur Pie"?'

'He did,' says Mum, going a bit red.

'Mmm-hmm. We have been in contact with the Food Safety Authority and it seems to be a very unusual case. Causing quite a stir in the medical community, I can tell you. Some sort of genetic meat experiment gone awry.'

Mum and I both nod.

'I imagine the newspapers will pick it up pretty soon. The gardaí are involved now,

I hear. We can't be having this kind of nonsense,' she says, waving in my general direction.

Mum starts to cough. Dr Shanahan looks up. 'Are you quite all right, Rebecca?'

'Yes, fine. Just a bit of a cough I can't shift.'

'I see. Are you taking anything for it?'

'Well, a cough bottle,' says Mum.

'I'll write you a prescription. We'll need to clear that up quickly,' says Dr Shanahan, focusing on her two-fingered typing again.

I can see Mum is getting flustered by this change of direction. She's fidgeting and moving about in her seat.

'The cat,' she says. 'The dinosaur cat.'

Dr Shanahan raises her eyebrows as she gives Mum another one of her over-the-glasses looks.

Mum tries to explain. 'Well, Rory found this dinosaur. We thought it was a gull but it was really a cat. It had eaten the pie too and this morning it became a cat again.'

Silence from Dr Shanahan. Mum goes quiet and fidgets. Dr Shanahan's silences have that effect.

A few long uncomfortable seconds later Dr Shanahan says, 'A cat?'

'A cat that was a dinosaur,' says Mum. 'This morning its feathers fell out and it turned back into a cat again.'

'Spontaneous re-transformation,' mutters Dr Shanahan. 'How interesting.'

'Do you think Rory might become himself again? Like the cat?' asks Mum hopefully.

IS THIS THE END?

'We still haven't found a cure for this,' says Dr Shanahan. 'But one can always hope.'

Then my brain does a thing. You know that thing when some quiet bit of your brain is working away connecting things without you even realising it and then it just pops up randomly with an answer? That thing. A lightning-bolt insight. Thank you, brain.

I hop over to the doctor's desk and start tapping my claws on the prescription the doctor has just written and then nudging Mum.

It takes her a bit, but she has had quite a lot of training in my brain jumps.

'Oh,' she says, 'I see, Rory. Yes. Yes, of course.'

She turns to Dr Shanahan. 'The cat had some of my cough medicine this morning a little while before it transformed. Do you think that could be the reason?'

'You gave the cat cough medicine?' Dr Shanahan asks slowly.

'Well, no, we didn't give it to him. He more, like, got it when we weren't looking, and it was a dinosaur then, not a cat.'

Dr Shanahan is looking confused.

'Well, it was the cat, but it was still a dinosaur when it drank the cough mixture and we didn't know it was a cat then,' says Mum.

I can see where I get my ability to explain things clearly.

More uncomfortable seconds pass. Then Dr Shanahan says, 'Well, I don't see any harm in Rory trying the cough medicine. I don't have anything else to offer him. Two spoons three times a day and let me know how you get on.'

She nods at us, then at the door. 'Thank you, Rebecca and Rory.'

And before we know it, we are outside the door.

Mum starts to cry. She does that when she's full of emotion. Then she takes a deep breath and puts an arm around me. 'It'll be fine, sweetie.'

I nod and we walk home.

No, this is the End

So the cough bottle does work – Burp found the cure! My transformation isn't as quick as Burp's. Over the next few days my tail and head get smaller, as do my claws. One morning I wake up and am surrounded by a pile of feathers and the last few fall out a day later. It is a weirdly uncomfortable and disturbing experience and I hide away until I feel like myself again.

We have a few nice chilled days at home, Mum and Burp and I. Mum is taking some time off work until I recover. Dr Shanahan gave her a sick note for her cough.

I'm not back to full gaming strength yet. It's taking a while for my fingers to get up

to power again, so I'm just having short goes on *Big Battle World*. But hurray for hands and opposable thumbs. Daria, Oleg and I are still planning to take down the Doom Boss. It just hasn't happened yet. We got slightly distracted by the whole Rory-turning-into-a-dinosaur thing.

Best news? Burp is staying with us. For ever. He is still an adorable wee savage beast, although he occasionally launches himself out the window and pesters Jebey to bring him back up to us. We were worried that some family might have lost him so we put pictures of him up around and contacted the local lost pets page, but Andy says he was a stray who had been hanging around for a bit. He's part of our weird little chaotic family now! Weird in the totally best way, obviously.

When I'm fully human, Mum decides we should have a recovery party. I invite Daria and Oleg and we have a catch-up on *Hawke Hill* while feasting on hot chocolate and those dinosaur-shaped biscuits with chocolate on one side. (Oleg's mum sent them over.) Mum makes us popcorn and eggy bread. (That's what we call French toast in our house.) But there are absolutely no sausages!

'Welcome back, Roary Rory,' says Oleg, doing a cheers with his hot chocolate as we watch the season two finale.

'Roar,' I roar.

'Somebody's voice box is much improved,' says Daria. Then she adds as Burp struts by, 'Do you know cats can either purr or roar? Like, small cats like Burp obviously purr and so do cheetahs but they can't roar and lions can't purr.'

'Aw, I want lions to be able to purr,' says Oleg. 'Rory, you make lions able to purr.'

'OK, Oleg, just for you,' I say. 'I will take my magic transformation cough medicine and feed it to the lions at the zoo and they will purr for Oleg.'

'Yeah,' says Oleg. 'Oleg happy.'

'That won't work,' says Daria, munching on popcorn.

I roll my eyes.

We silly.

'You coming to school Monday?' Daria asks.

I look at Mum. She nods. I sigh.

'Yup,' I say. 'One-Two and I have missed each other. I'm looking forward to giving him a big squishy hug, and to him telling me how he has missed my witty jokes.'

Daria and Oleg are snorting laughing.

'Well, you will be devastated to hear that

he is going on a career break,' says Daria. 'No more One-Two this term!'

'Too many one-star reviews,' says Oleg.

'Dave, the substitute teacher, is OK. Although he likes to start the day with us all doing star jumps and singing the "Everyone Is so Absolutely Awesome" song,' says Daria, when she gets her breath back.

Oleg and I give a thumbs-down to star jumps and singing, but Dave does sound a lot better than One-Two.

Laura and Tina, who's now a kid, arrive and I have to introduce myself because they haven't met me in human-mode.

'Well, you make quite an adorable human too!' says Laura laughing, but it is totally not funny and I am not impressed at my so-called friends giggling and snorting on the couch.

'Thanks so much for letting us all know about the cough medicine cure,' says Laura to Mum.

'Oh, it was Rory figured it out,' says Mum.

'Actually, it was Burp,' I say. 'Do you want to watch *Hawke Hill* with us? I can catch you up on the story so far.'

'No, thanks,' says Laura. 'But Tina might sit with ye for a bit while your mum and I chat. Oh, and your mum asked me to give you the details of the athletics club that Tina goes to. There are loads of kids your age there and there are hurdles and relay as well as just running.'

Lex even pops by the party for a bit. I think Mum invited him. He's all chat and excitement. Nah, I'm joking. He's all Lex. He sits on the armchair with his big legs and his big black boots stretching in front of him, with Burp curled up on his lap. He has a mug of hot chocolate with extra marshmallows in his hand, which he raises in a silent salute to me. Then he watches *Hawke Hill* with us for a bit.

When he gets up to go, he mutters about going to work.

'Did you get a new job, Lex?' asks Mum.

He grunts affirmatively and mumbles, 'Garden centre.'

'Good for you,' says Mum.

As he leaves, I notice something very weird. Our Lex of the all-in-black gothiness is wearing a jumper that is actually not black at all, but a very very very dark green. For once, I decide not to say anything.

ONE MORE THING

Oh, I haven't told you about Andy, you know, the security guard, Daria's brother. He turned out to be a secret hero. Not the cape-and-underpants-over-tights kind. That would just be weird.

So, he's not a fan of Shane, Manager, and didn't like how he treated us. In fact, not only did he not like Shane, he was very suspicious of him. When Shane went off shift Andy got the bag he had taken from us out of the skip again, and he went through the memos in it, which detailed Shane's dealings with a very dodgy pie company, which was using 'top secret' technology to produce cheap meat for pies. Using dinosaur DNA. Do they not watch movies? How was that ever going to end well?

So, Andy brought the manky memos and the bag of old pies to the garda station and Shane is having to answer some very serious questions and is no longer a team member at BuyMart.

I NEARLY FORGOT TO TELL YOU

The local paper, *The Insidious Whisperer*, called Mum and wanted to do an article, or a 'piece' they call it, on recent events, meaning the dinosaur stuff. Mum said OK if they don't mention my name. They even quoted Daria as 'a local dinosaur expert'. We are never going to hear the end of this.

They wanted a photograph of me in dino-mode so Daria sent one from her phone that Oleg took of me and Burp, when we were skip hunting. You won't believe it but they put it on their social media and it has gone viral. Like, proper viral, and Oleg is

totally losing it (in a good way) because
he is given photo credit and he now has
thousands of Likes.

'Living the dream, Rory,' he says, as if I'm interviewing him rather than us having a conversation on the half wall, while we wait for Daria. 'My parents are even thinking of buying me a camera so that I can develop my photography skills. I'm telling them that phone cameras are the best, but it could be an uphill struggle, Rory, an uphill struggle. In the meantime ...' He points his two index fingers at me.

'Like and Subscribe,' I say, giving a thumbs-up.

THE LAST THING, I PROMISE

Weirdest of all, sometimes I'll just be doing ordinary stuff and suddenly my hearing gets very sharp and I get a prickly feeling like feathers are starting to grow, but I just take a spoon of the cough medicine and everything stays normal. Well, our version of normal anyway.

We go to see Dr Shanahan a week after my recovery and she says there is now a whole department in the university researching 'Our Incident'.

'It is changing our perceptions of DNA and genetic manipulation,' she says, as she raises one eyebrow at me, which I think means she is really excited about this.

As I explain about the weird feeling, she pauses her two-fingered typing.

'I would recommend you carry a dose of that cough medicine on your person at all times. Treat it like an asthma inhaler or an EpiPen,' she says. Then she does her looking-over-the-top-of-her-glasses thing at me. 'At all times!'

'Or what?' I say.

'Or nothing, Rory,' she says sternly. 'We are never going to find out, sure we aren't? Rory?'

I shake my head. 'Carry medicine all the time, got it,' I say, giving her a thumbs-up.

I don't tell her that Burp has gone dino-mode on us a few times but a drop of cough mixture brings him back to his furry self.

There is no need for Dr Shanahan or all those university people to know that. That is just between Burp, Mum and me.

ABOUT THE AUTHOR

Jen writes stories and poetry, for both children and grown-ups. She loves to write neurodivergent characters so people like her can see themselves in books. She lives by the sea with her family and their cats, goats, chickens and rabbit.

Jen has wanted to be a writer since she was very small, although she also wanted to be a superhero, a firefighter and the President of Ireland. You can find her at www.jenwallacecreates.ie and @jenwallacecreates on Instagram.

ABOUT THE ILLUSTRATOR

Alan is tall. Very tall.

He writes and illustrates children's books. But that is a work in progress.

The tallness is permanent. Hopefully.

Alan lives with his family beside the sea in the northeast of Ireland.

Find out more and subscribe at www.spoiltchild.com

ACKNOWLEDGEMENTS

Thank you to all at Little island, to Siobhán for your encouragement and kind words, to Matthew for taking a chance on Rory and me, and to Kate and Elizabeth for your patience and guidance. It has been a pleasure working with you all.

Thank you to Alan for the fabulous artwork.

Thank you to Children's Books Ireland, particularly Aoife and Elaina, and all involved in the Raising Voices Fellowship: Illustrators Ireland, Publishing Ireland, The Tyrone Guthrie Centre, Dublin Book Festival and the Arts Council, mentors Celine Kiernan and Catherine Ann Cullen. You all welcomed me and guided me gently and I will be forever grateful. Thank you to the RV Fellows, Nene, Carol, Aileen, Conor and Kate, for the support and antics.

Thank you to my family and friends, to Mum, Dad, Christine and Stephen, all my amazing support network.

Neil, thank you for all the things, always.

To everyone who took the time to read my work and feedback on it, Dee, Martin and Caia, thank you.

If I have omitted you here it is due to my scattiness and please know that it will haunt me.

ABOUT LITTLE ISLAND

Little Island is an award-winning independent Irish publisher of books for young readers, founded in 2010 by Ireland's first Laureate na nÓg (children's laureate), Siobhán Parkinson. Little Island books are found throughout Ireland, the UK, North America, and in translation around the world. You can find out more at littleisland.ie

RECENT AWARDS FOR LITTLE ISLAND BOOKS

Youth Libraries Group Publisher of the Year 2023

IBBY Honour List 2024
The Táin by Alan Titley, illus. by Eoin Coveney
Things I Know by Helena Close

An Post Irish Book Awards:
Teen and YA Book of the Year 2023
Black and Irish: Legends, Trailblazers & Everyday Heroes by Leon Diop and Briana Fitzsimons, illus. by Jessica Louis

An Post Irish Book Awards:
Children's Book of the Year (Senior) 2023
I Am the Wind: Irish Poems for Children Everywhere ed. by Sarah Webb and Lucinda Jacob, illus. by Ashwin Chacko

White Raven Award 2023
Carnegie Medal for Writing shortlist 2023
YA Book Prize shortlist 2023
Kirkus Prize finalist 2023
The Eternal Return of Clara Hart by Louise Finch

Literacy Association of Ireland Biennial Book Awards:
Age 10–13 Award 2023
USBBY Outstanding International Books List 2023
Spark! School Book Award: Fiction Age 9+ Award 2022
Wolfstongue by Sam Thompson, illus. by Anna Tromop